This Walker book belongs to:

_____

_____

_____

First published 1986 by Walker Books Ltd
87 Vauxhall Walk, London SE11 5HJ
This edition published 2011

2 4 6 8 10 9 7 5 3 1

Text © 1986 Allan Ahlberg
Illustrations © 1986 Colin McNaughton

This book has been typeset in New Baskerville Educational

Printed in China

British Library Cataloguing in Publication Data:
a catalogue record for this book is available from the British Library

ISBN 978-1-4063-3368-8

www.walker.co.uk

Tell Us A Story

Allan Ahlberg
Colin McNaughton

WALKER BOOKS
AND SUBSIDIARIES
LONDON · BOSTON · SYDNEY · AUCKLAND

Contents

The Pig

Two little boys
climbed up to bed.

'Tell us a story, Dad,'
they said.

'Right!' said Dad.
'There was once a pig
who ate too much
and got so big
he couldn't sit down,
he couldn't bend...

So he ate standing up
and got bigger – The End!'

The Cat

'That story's no good, Dad,'
the little boys said.
'Tell us a better one instead.'

'Right!' said Dad.
'There was once a cat
who ate too much
and got so fat

he split his fur
which he had to mend
with a sewing machine
and a zip – The End!'

The Horse

'That story's too mad, Dad,'
the little boys said.

'Tell us another one instead.'

'Right!' said Dad.
'There was once a horse
who ate too much
and died, of course –

The End.'

The Cow

'That story's too sad, Dad,'
  the little boys said.
'Tell us a happier one instead.'

Right…

'Right…' said Dad.
'There was once a cow
who ate so much
that even now

she fills two fields

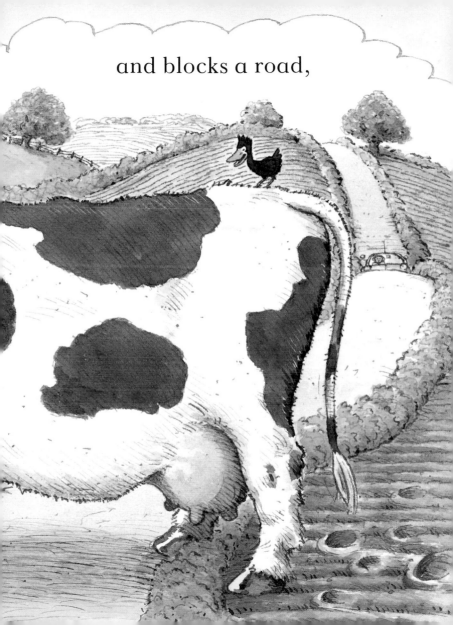

and blocks a road,

and when they milk her
she has to be towed!

She wins gold cups
and medals too,
for the creamiest milk
and the *loudest* moo!

Moo!

Now that's the end,'
said Dad. 'No more.'
And he shut his eyes
and began to snore.

Then the two little boys
climbed out of bed
and crept downstairs...

to their Mum instead.

The End